I Want To Make Friends

A Book for Preschoolers, Kindergartners, and their Parents

Written by B. Annye Rothenberg, Ph.D.
Child/Parent Psychologist

Illustrated by
Bonnie Bright

REDWOOD CITY, CALIFORNIA

DEDICATION

To the many parents who do all they can - and even more - to raise their children well.

And to my grown-up son, Bret, *who is so knowledgeable about so many things and who patiently guides those of us lucky enough to have him in our lives. – B.A.R.*

I'd like to thank my family for the wonderful support through this tough, yet rewarding year of illustrating three books at once! A special thanks also goes out to Annye for choosing me to be her illustrator. – B.B.

Text copyright © 2012 by B. Annye Rothenberg
Illustrations copyright © 2012 by Bonnie Bright

Library of Congress Control Number: 2011919081
ISBN: 978-0-9790420-4-1(pbk.)

Printed in China.   First printing May 2012
10 9 8 7 6 5 4 3 2 1

Published by
PERFECTING PARENTING PRESS
REDWOOD CITY, CALIFORNIA
www.PerfectingParentingPress.com

To order by phone, call:
(810) 388-9500 (M-F 9-5 ET)
For other questions, call:
(650) 275-3809 (M-F 8-5 PT)

Children's book in collaboration with
SuAnn and Kevin Kiser
Palo Alto, California

Parents' manual edited by
Caroline Grannan
San Francisco, California

Book design by
Cathleen O'Brien,
A Book in the Hand
San Francisco, California

• WHAT'S IN THIS BOOK FOR CHILDREN AND FOR PARENTS •

This fifth book in a series focuses on the challenges of guiding young children to learn how to get along with other youngsters. Most parents have to teach their preschool-age children to become skilled playmates. Even many kindergartners are still developing social skills.

The first part of this book is a meaningful and realistic story that helps three- through six-year-olds understand how to make friends. The second part is a comprehensive guidance manual for parents (and their advisers, such as pediatricians and teachers). *Together, the children's story and the parents' manual help you learn to guide your child to build successful friendships and what to do when he or she is having social difficulties.*

The children's story shows what happens when Zachary, like other youngsters, wants his preschool classmates to always do what he says. Zachary's teachers and parents help him learn how that bothers kids and how to play with them so he can have friends and be liked.

Section One of the parents' manual explains how your child can become comfortable around other children. Section Two provides tools to use at home so your child is better prepared to be a friend.*Section Three explains the three most common unfriendly patterns children may develop (being bossy, persistently annoying, or physically aggressive) and the two most common uncomfortable patterns (being quiet and self-conscious or thin-skinned and easily upset). This section guides parents in changing their child's and even his playmate's behavior.* Section Four explains how to help an "only" child *and* a child who has difficult sibling relations overcome those challenges and develop good peer skills. The Parents' Guide includes real-life examples and concludes with a summary of practical guidelines.

— Annye Rothenberg, Ph.D., *Child/Parent Psychologist*

On Friday, Daddy dropped me off at preschool. "Have fun, Zachary," he said.

"I'll try," I said.

I went over to the block corner. Lamar and Sheng were building a tower. I wanted them to play with me.

I took a long block from Lamar's hand. "Can I have this?" I asked.

"Hey!" said Lamar. "I'm using that for the tower."

"I have a better idea," I said. "We should make a barn, OK guys?"

"No," said Lamar.

"We're not going to play with you, Zachary." said Sheng.

I built blocks by myself until it was cleanup time.

Everyone started putting away toys.

"Zachary," said Teacher Sara, "we need your help, too."

"I hardly played with anything, so I don't have to help with cleanup," I said.

"Time to wash our hands," Teacher Maribel said.

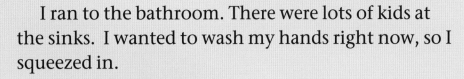

I ran to the bathroom. There were lots of kids at the sinks. I wanted to wash my hands right now, so I squeezed in.

"Ow!" said Ronit.

"Stop it," said Lamar.

"I was here before you," said Sheng.

"I'm telling the teacher," said Lilly.

"Zachary," said Teacher Sara, "what's going on?"

"I have to wash my hands," I said.

"Everyone does," said Teacher Sara. "But it's not OK to push the other kids out of the way. You have to wait your turn."

I waited a long time.

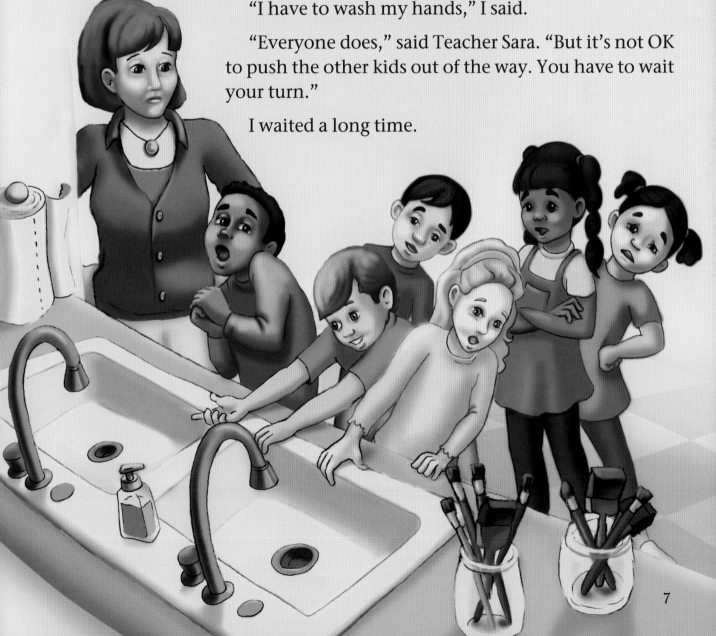

After snack, I went to the sandbox to dig. Juan and Anisha were there.

"Anisha," said Juan, "I'm going to dig a deep hole. Do you want to dig with me?"

"No," said Anisha. "I want to fill up my pail with sand and make a castle."

"If you help me dig a hole," said Juan, "we can use the sand to make your castle."

"OK," said Anisha. "I like that idea."

"I have an even better idea," I said.

"Oh no!" said Anisha.

"Let's go on the play structure," said Juan. They ran off.

I went to Teacher Maribel. "No one wants to play with me," I said.

"What makes you think that?" asked Teacher Maribel.

"When I say I have a better idea, they won't listen."

"Next time, try asking, 'What can I do to help?' " said Teacher Maribel.

"But my ideas are better," I said.

"They thought their ideas were very good."

"They did?"

Later, when I was sitting on the swing, Teacher Sara said, "Zachary, what's the matter?"

"I have no friends," I said.

"If you want friends," said Teacher Sara, "you need to learn how to be a good friend. One way is to tell people what you like about what they are doing."

"Do I have to do that?" I asked.

"You do if you want friends," said Teacher Sara.

When Mommy picked me up from school, she asked, "Did you have fun today?"

"A little," I said. "But no one wants to play with me." I was happy that tomorrow was the start of an extra long weekend.

On Saturday morning, Mommy said, "Daddy and I had a good talk on the phone with Teacher Maribel last night. Now we have some new ways to help you make friends."

"When I get back from my errands," said Daddy, "I'll have time to play with you."

"Mommy, will you play with me now?" I asked. "I want to do the fire station puzzle."

"You're old enough that you shouldn't always get to decide what we play," said Mommy. "I'll choose what we play first, and then you'll have a turn. I'd like us to play soccer now."

"But my idea is better," I said.

"When someone says their idea is better than mine, it hurts my feelings and makes me angry," said Mommy. "I don't want to play with someone who makes me feel that way. I'll play with you after I do the dishes and clean the bathroom."

I colored by myself
for a long time.

Then, Mommy and I played soccer and did the puzzle together. Mommy's idea was as good as mine!

When Daddy got home, I asked, "Can we play now?"

"Yes," said Daddy, "but it's my turn to pick what we do. Let's play catch with the baseball."

"How about if we play catch first," I said, "and then we build with blocks."

"I like that," said Daddy.

We played for awhile. "I can play better than you," I said.

"That's not a kind thing to say," said Daddy, "and I don't want to play with anyone who's not being nice to me."

"But I'm having fun," I said, "and I don't want to stop playing." I thought very hard, and then said, "We're both very good ballplayers."

Daddy smiled. "That's much better."

After a while, we went inside and built a bridge with my blocks.

"Dinner is almost ready," called Mommy. "Time to clean up your toys and wash your hands."

"You have to help me," I told Daddy.

"I'll put away the baseball," said Daddy, "but you need to put away the other things you played with."

I put away my toys and went to wash my hands. Daddy was already at the sink holding the soap. I took it from him and said, "Can I have that?"

"Don't grab the soap," said Daddy. "Ask if you can use it when I'm done."

"Let's try that over," said Mommy. "I'll call you to dinner again, and you can practice being polite."

Soon Mommy said, "Dinner is ready!"

This time I said, "Daddy, can I please have the soap when you're done?"

Daddy smiled. "You sure can."

It was fun practicing being a good friend with Mommy and Daddy all weekend.

On Tuesday morning, the kids at preschool had lots to tell the teachers. I listened carefully. When it was my turn, I told about playing soccer and baseball.

Later, Lamar, Juan, and Sheng were playing with blocks.

"What are you building?" I asked.

"A race track," said Juan.

"That sounds like fun," I said. "What can I do to help?"

"You want to help?" asked Lamar.

"Yes, I do."

"OK," said Sheng.

While we played together, I listened to their ideas. I told them one of mine, but I didn't say that my idea was better. We all had fun.

21

Then I saw Ronit, Lilly, and Anisha doing Play-Doh. I sat at the table and used a shape cutter to make a dinosaur.

"I like your giraffe," I said to Ronit. Ronit smiled.

"That's an awesome dinosaur, Zachary," said Lilly.

"Thanks," I said. "What are you making, Anisha?"

"A whale," said Anisha. "Would you like to use the whale shape?"

"Yes," I said, "I would."

When Teacher Maribel said it was cleanup time,
I helped a lot.

At bathroom time, I waited in line. Sheng, Lamar, and Juan were talking about what they did over the weekend.

Sheng said, "I went on a bike ride."

"I helped plant the garden," said Lamar.

"I went to a fair," said Juan. "Zachary, what did you do on the weekend?"

"I practiced being a good friend," I said.

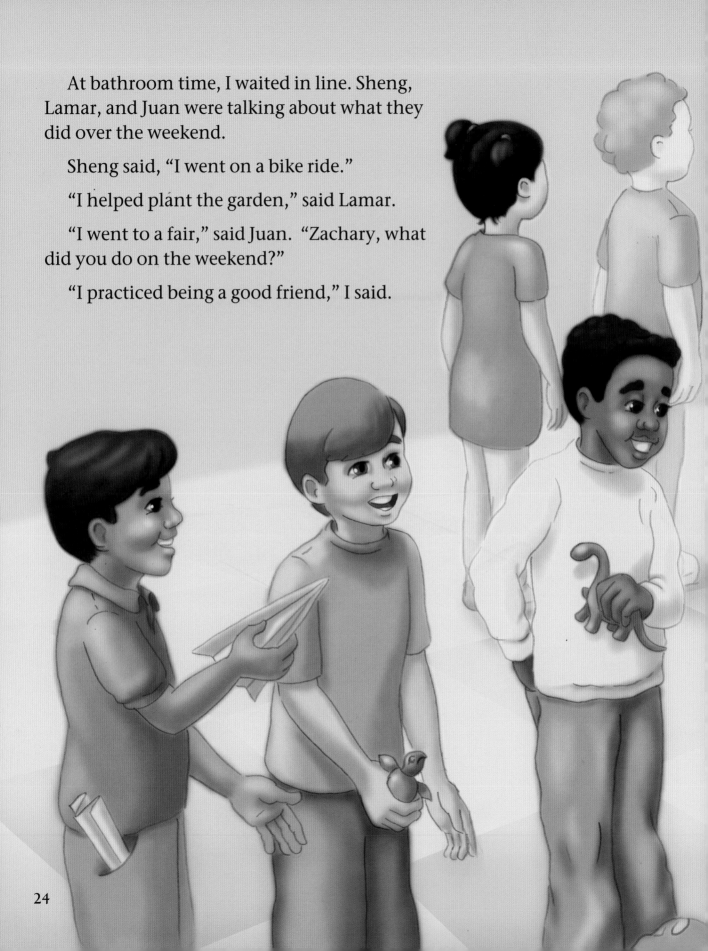

"You really are a better friend today, Zachary," said Lamar.

"You're fun to play with now," said Sheng.

"Thanks," I said. I smiled at my new friends and they smiled back at me. Now I can't wait to go to preschool every day.

A GUIDANCE SECTION FOR PARENTS

• INTRODUCTION •

Learning how to play with other children is a prelude to one of the most important life skills: getting along with others. Children who don't play well with others are lonely and isolated, and are less likely to enjoy preschool, day care, elementary school, and other social settings. This parents' guidance manual will provide specific approaches to help your child become socially skilled, as well as guiding you when your child or her[1] peers have unfriendly and/or uncomfortable socializing patterns.

These skills usually take years to learn. Kids benefit most when parents know how to teach friendship skills. Preschool and kindergarten teachers are usually trained to help your children become socially skilled. Your child's teachers will welcome your partnership, knowledge, and skills in working on these issues.

[1]To avoid the awkward use of "he/she," the sections in this guide will alternate between both.

HOW TO BE SURE YOUR CHILD HAS ENOUGH CONTACT WITH OTHER YOUNG CHILDREN

Make sure that your young children have enough time with other little children to become comfortable with them. Take them to parks, small playgroups, and classes such as gym and art. *One-on-one playdates are especially helpful.* If your child rarely spends time with peers – seeing them only briefly once or twice a week – he will likely develop social skills more slowly.

PRESCHOOLS AND CHILD CARE OPTIONS

As children get close to three years old, preschool is almost always a useful socializing, learning, and independence-building experience. Preschools are designed for children ages two and three-quarters up to kindergarten age, and are typically about three or four hours each session, two to five days a week. Whether the preschool is play-based or more academic, be sure the preschool teachers can help the children develop social skills.

Another option is the child care center, which offers all-day care and is used primarily when both parents work full-time. It's best *not* to keep a child in day care for the maximum hours possible. The ten-hour day that most child care centers operate is generally considered too long to leave a child five days a week. Consider staggering your work hours with your spouse's so your child is with you more. Extra time with your child means more time to enjoy each other, less stress from time pressure and fatigue, *and* more opportunity to notice and help with *any* developing issues.

The year before kindergarten, children should go to preschool five days a week. If your preschool is play-based, find out if it offers some activities to prepare the kids for kindergarten – or consider finding a class or activity with more structure, demands, teacher-directed activities, *and* some emphasis on academics. (*Talk to your child's pre-K teacher and the elementary school principal or kindergarten teacher to find out how to prepare her academically, behaviorally, and socially for kindergarten.*)

• SECTION TWO •

USEFUL TOOLS FOR ALL PARENTS TEACHING THEIR KIDS SOCIAL SKILLS

Along with providing enough time and experience with peers, there are other ways to improve children's skill at making friends.

HOW TO PLAY WITH YOUR YOUNGSTERS

If your child always gets to choose what to play when you're playing with him, he may expect to always decide the activity when he's with parents *and* peers. The child who expects to be in charge and gets resistance from a playmate may be surprised, frustrated, and angry. He may insist on his way. Or he may feel rejected, shut down, and just play by himself. It's wise for any parents playing with their child to take turns deciding what to play, especially once a child is about two and a half years old. Children shouldn't be able to **run the play even when it is their turn**. Children may want to dismantle what you're still building or tell you what character to play or what words to say. All of this leads to problematic assumptions of how peer (or parent-child) play should go. **The guideline to remember is: Don't let your child do anything in playing with you that wouldn't work if he tried it with a peer.**

TELL HER HOW HER BEHAVIOR AFFECTS YOU

It is also important in **all** your interactions with your child – not just playtime – to let her know if something she says or does bothers you. **It's also helpful to let her know why she just said or did that**. For example, if she keeps shouting louder and louder when you are talking to someone else, tell her: "I know you want me to notice you, but when you shout while I'm talking to Grandma, I get very annoyed and then I don't want to talk to you." Then tell her what she could say that would be acceptable to you: **"Mom (Dad), when you have a minute, I want to tell you something."**

Or if you announce that it's time to pick up the toys and she says, "You're a mean poopy head," let her know why you think she's saying that and why you're not going to be able to be with her for a while. Then have her

practice what she should have said: "Mommy, it makes me mad when you tell me to clean up my toys." Just telling her how you feel about what she just said or did isn't enough to change behavior (e.g., "That makes me sad"). **Not being available to her for a while is a useful consequence, and so is having her practice better behavior – several times in a row.**

We need to tell our child if her behavior annoys, angers, or saddens us. Otherwise, she is more likely to be self-centered, less empathetic, and less able to control her unlikeable behavior – now and in the future.

TEACHING A CHILD HOW TO TAKE TURNS IN CONVERSATION

Most young children do not naturally understand about taking turns in conversations. Many just keep talking and talking. We may find ourselves checking out mentally, giving our kids only half-attention. But if we don't teach children to let others talk, it's harder for peers to want to be with our child. As we know, friendships for children four and older are largely based on verbal communication, not just activities like chasing each other.

If your child is developing the habit of nonstop talking, say something like, "Hey, I don't want to just listen. I have something I want to say" (or "ask you about"). Then take your turn. As he goes back to too much talking, tell him to ask you if you want to hear any more about that. **Make sure you say no at least half the time.** Tell him about something, but take breaks to ask him if he wants to hear more. That models more sensitive and respectful communication.

Also teach him to ask you questions like "How was your day, Daddy?" "What happened today, Mommy?" Teach him to say something complimentary about you – "I like your shirt, shoes, etc." – and to do that with kids as well. Teach him to ask the kids questions: "Did you get an owie?" when they have a Band-aid – and to share something relevant: "I fell off my scooter and got a scrape, but it's better now." You can make some of these suggestions quietly to him when he's going to school or playdates. *Incorporating empathetic turn-taking into your interaction with him is more effective than just telling him how to behave.*

HELPING YOUR CHILD PRACTICE ESSENTIAL PEER PLAY SKILLS

You can role-play common peer situations with your child. Let her in on what you're trying so she understands that you're not being mean. When your child asks you to play something like blocks or house, you should sometimes say, "I don't want to do that now." If your child is stuck, you can say, "I want to do a puzzle." Then see what she does next. You can also say (because you're the parent, not her peer), *"Can you think of something I really like to do?"* This helps your child increase her skills in getting kids to play with her – as well as increasing her empathy. This will give her more ways to get into peer play as well as handle rejection.

Also ignore her sometimes when she asks you to play and see if she knows what to do. Show her that she should repeat what she said a little louder or more enthusiastically, or touch your arm. Kids can learn to modify their play idea to make it sound like more fun. Remember that saying "Can I play?" often gets a "no" response unless an adult is standing there.

Try getting another family member to join the play, and both of you ignore your child. She'll probably get mad and say something like, "Hey, you were playing with me!" Try getting her to practice saying, "Hey, do you want to play too? Cool!" You can also all have fun by talking for puppets and stuffed animals as you teach your child social skills.

TEACHING PLAY SKILLS WHEN YOUR CHILD IS WITH OTHER KIDS

Teach him to say to kids, "Do you want to play? Let's go on the slide," etc. Or "I'm Jonas – what's your name?" Prompt him on playdates and at the park or playgroup.

Although practicing taking turns and sharing with parents is helpful, it's much harder with another child. So you'll still need to teach him *when* he's playing with peers. You can teach your child that he needs to let Cole have a turn with his toy for two minutes. Set a timer (or look at your watch) and make another toy (or activity) seem interesting to the child who's waiting. Even if the child waiting loses interest, keep your word and return the toy to him. Teach the kids to say, "I'll give you a turn in two minutes." Or, "Can I have a turn with that in five minutes?" (Or "...when you're done with it?") Although young children don't have a sense of time, you can be the time-watcher. As they become kindergartners, peers will feel more sure about getting their turn after the promised length of time.

Children may stop playing with each other after just a little while. One child may switch activities or start playing with another child. Preschoolers don't often alert their playmates to what they're doing. If your child is commonly left or if he seems sad about this turn of events, you can have him suggest another idea. For example, both kids were digging in the sand and one leaves and climbs on the play structure. You could suggest to your child that he look for the other child, then go to the play structure and say something like, "Do you want to climb together or do you want to swing with me?" Teach him that if the other child says no, he can say, "What do you want to do (or play)?"

Kids have to learn to deal with being ignored or rejected. Kids may say, "I don't want to play with you," or even, "Go away." It's usually worthwhile to teach our kids to make another attempt by suggesting an idea in an enthusiastic, confident way (the manner we would use when we're trying to talk them into something). For a child, this could be, "Let's climb the play structure and try to cross the bridge" or "How about if we take our cars and race them in the tunnel?" If that doesn't work, they can say, "Maybe later," or ask another child to play.

WHEN A PLAYDATE FALLS APART

When we have a playmate over and our child doesn't want to play with her anymore, it's difficult to salvage the situation. If your child goes to her room or says she wants her playdate to go home, first try to figure out what caused the breakdown. *If it can't be resolved, you can set up activities that are easy to share: Play-Doh; water play at adjacent sinks or in a big container outdoors; or digging in the sandbox.* If necessary, you can read to them or do a science or cooking project with both, or have them sit with you for a snack. If your child still retreats to her room, you'll need to find something to do with the visiting child. As a last resort, if there are hours left till the end of this playdate, you'll have to call the other parent to pick up the child.

When your child should have a consequence and the playdate is still there, explain the situation to both kids and proceed with the consequence. You'll need to spend time with the visiting youngster, because she's likely to be very uncomfortable while your child is in time-out or having any consequence. At times, you may also need to give some consequence to the playmate or both – the visitor and your child. Rather than avoiding the consequence, give it and explain later to the other parent. If your child-rearing approach makes sense to the other parent, this may work out. *We need to establish that we have the same rules and standards for all kids when we're in charge.*

WHAT TO DO WHEN YOUR CHILD SAYS, "NO ONE WANTS TO PLAY WITH ME"

Many children tell their parents, "I don't have any friends"; "Everyone is mean to me"; or, "No one wants to play with me." Responding with empathy is a good start – e.g., "Sounds like you had a hard day (an unhappy day)" – and see what else your child can tell you. If the "no friends" comments are frequent, find out what your child's teacher has noticed.

Teach your child that most kids are nice but won't act nice if someone takes away their toys or tries to be their boss. If your child does something that wasn't nice, encourage him to tell you what he did. This is to help him see his role, so he's aware of what made the other child not want to play with him. Since this is hard for a young child to understand, tell him about times in your childhood when you and a classmate weren't nice to each other.

When your child tells you he doesn't have any friends, try not to blame him or the other children. If your child, age four to six, is upset about an incident, try to get him to give details. Try not to give advice too soon, but instead see if he can figure out what he could have done so neither child would be mad or sad. When he complains that kids are treating him badly, it's an opportunity for him to learn how to develop friendships and solve peer problems. Keep trying to help him see the other child's perspective as well as his, not just blame others. Even when your child is doing well socially, you will both encounter many kids whose behavior will be challenging. The next section teaches you how to guide your child and his playmates.

• SECTION THREE •

WHAT YOU CAN DO WHEN YOUR KIDS HAVE UNFRIENDLY OR UNCOMFORTABLE WAYS OF BEHAVING WITH PEERS

While labeling children is often not desirable, **children with social difficulties do fall into certain patterns**. This section looks at five of the most common problematic patterns, and how to help young children overcome these difficulties so they can become socially skilled.

Three of the patterns fall into the category of children who are bothersome to others:

- Bossy children (p. 30)
- Annoying children (p. 32)
- Physically aggressive children (p. 34)

Two of the patterns fall into the category *of children who are uncertain with other youngsters and have difficulty standing up for themselves:*

- Quiet, self-conscious children (p. 37)
- Thin-skinned, very sensitive children (p. 40)

You should consider **which type of child most resembles your own.** Read that section to learn the skills to help your child. Guiding your child to become more socially skilled will take time and patience, effort, and consistency, but it will be worth it.

THE BOSSY CHILD: *"YOU HAVE TO DO WHAT I SAY!"*

HOW DO THESE CHILDREN BEHAVE?

These youngsters tell the other children what to do **or** not do. Tucker and Brandon are playing with blocks. Tucker is giving Brandon orders: "Don't put that that there. You have to put it here." Or: "It goes this way. You're not doing it right." Often, these controlling children give directions that don't make sense. Their playmates may end up just standing there because the "controller" says everything they do is "wrong." Most often, the children being controlled just drift away. Some controlling children try to turn the other kids into servants. Tucker might order Brandon: "Get me one red block and two blue blocks right now."

By kindergarten age, peers start resisting: "You're not the boss of me. I can make it how I want. I'm not going to do what you say." That leaves the "controller" without kids to boss, but also without the skills he needs to have friends. Playing with a controller is a frustrating and sometimes demeaning experience for peers, and both the controller and the controlled child need guidance.

WHAT CAN YOU DO AT THE MOMENT?[2]

Tucker is attempting to control Brandon's play. Here's a way to work with both children to help them interact successfully.

> Tucker: *You have to put the block there.*
>
> Tucker's parent: *That's not being a good friend, Tucker. Brandon has good ideas too. Where do you want to put the block, Brandon?*
>
> or
>
> Tucker's parent (to Brandon): *You don't have to do what Tucker says. You don't have to put the red block on the blue block. Where do you want to put the red block?*

It's very important to do this, because most young children assume you will agree with your child instead of helping make the situation better for them. Brandon needs you to model for him how to deal with Tucker.

2 If parents of more than one child are involved or present, discuss **which** parent will guide the kids.

> Brandon: *Let's take these red blocks and build a tower over here.*
>
> Tucker: *No! I want to build a road right here.*
>
> Tucker's parent: *Tucker, both you and Brandon have good ideas. Nobody wants to only do what someone else says. Brandon, tell Tucker, "I want to build a tower now."*
>
> Brandon: *I want to build a tower.*
>
> Tucker's parent (to Brandon): *Tell Tucker, "We can do it together."*
>
> Brandon: *Let's build the tower together.*
>
> Tucker: *NO!*
>
> Parent (to Tucker): *I know this is hard for you, because you want to tell Brandon what to do, but you're not the boss of Brandon. Ask Brandon, "Do you want to build a tower and a road?" Let's see if Brandon wants to.*
>
> Tucker: *Do you?*
>
> Brandon: *OK.*

Work with the children as each struggles to practice what he needs to. If Tucker is unwilling to learn and resists your teaching **and** Brandon's ideas, you'll probably have to give Tucker a time-out and let Brandon play on his own **or** with you.

> Tucker's parent (to Tucker): *Brandon liked your idea. Now he wants to play with you. Let's ask him if he wants to work on the road or the tower first.*
>
> Brandon: *I want to build the road.*
>
> Tucker's parent (to Tucker): *Now tell Brandon, "You have good ideas too."*

The controller, Tucker, needs to learn that he can't just command and control, and has to find other ways to talk to and play with other youngsters. He needs to acknowledge that other kids have good ideas and be willing to play their ideas. Brandon needs encouragement to assert himself. ***You should use the same approach if the visiting child behaves like Tucker and your child***

acts like Brandon. Parents can work to effectively help their child's playmates. *It would be best to discuss these ideas with the other child's parents to make sure they find them acceptable. It's most effective teaching your child and his playdate when only one child's parent is doing it – otherwise the children will be confused by the differences.*

WHY KIDS BEHAVE THAT WAY

Usually, these children have lots of social energy and a tendency to be persistent, even relentless. They often have loud voices. Most of these characteristics are in-born. Some controlling children model themselves after a very commanding and directive parent or caregiver, or a domineering sibling. Conversely, other controlling children's parents may be uncertain in their parenting and too likely to give in. That child, who gets his way every time he pushes back, may think he can run the show with his parents and then, of course, with kids.

WHAT PARENTS CAN ADJUST IN THEIR RELATIONSHIP WITH THEIR CONTROLLING CHILD

What can you as a parent do at home (even when no peers are over) to help your child be less controlling with his peers?

• **Listen to how you talk to him – especially when you want him to do something *or* stop doing something.** Parents find themselves asking their kids repeatedly to get dressed, pick up their toys, say please and on and on. There are many ways to ask children. Just giving

orders and commands such as "stop playing and pick up your toys now" tends to frustrate and anger children and increase their resistance. Some parents move directly to threats or consequences when their children don't immediately obey. Today's parenting discourages controlling children in a harsh and disrespectful way – so check to see if you're modeling over-controlling.

• **Listening to your interactions may show you that rather than over-controlling, you're offering your preschooler too much say and you sound too uncertain.** If you say "Are you ready to pick up your toys?" and get resistance, do you let it go, and pick the toys up yourself? When you say it's almost time to go to the market, and your child stalls, do you decide it's too hard to get cooperation and you'll just go later? Then your child is likely to see himself as being in charge, and may become bossy to his peers. If this is your parenting style, you'll need to modify it so you become the leader. Children need to feel we mean what we say – we have good reasons and we don't cave in.

If your child feels not just in charge but free to be rude to you, work on his unacceptable behavior such as boasting that he's smarter than you. Tell him that makes you annoyed. Have him practice better actions and better words several times in a row. (*You need to tell your child how his poor behavior affects you, but that's not enough. Practicing better behavior helps him internalize it.*)

• **Notice how other parents get their children to do what they're told.** The approach described in the book ***Why Do I Have To?*** by this author helps parents get cooperation from young children in a way that's not too harsh nor too soft. The book tells how to make requests that motivate your child rather than warning him that his (natural preschool) defiance will be punished. For example: "Pretty soon, it will be time to pick up your toys so you can have time to use the paper cup with the holes in it in your bath."

• **See if one of your children is dominating the other in a way that seems insulting and almost paralyzing.** For example, Sam frequently tells Jasper: "Don't touch that. You're doing it wrong. Wait until I tell you where to put the block." Sam's frequent dominating behavior is likely to have a negative effect on Jasper's

personality. Monitor them closely and teach both how to behave toward each other. "Controller" Sam needs to learn to give up control and not insult Jasper, and he may need to talk to you about his feelings toward Jasper. Teach Jasper how to respond, including, "Mommy and Daddy said I have to tell them when you're mean to me." The dominating sib is usually older, but not always, because personality and temperament play a big role. (See pp. 42-44 for more guidance on sibling relations.)

• **Pay attention to your spouse's style.** Parents' styles need to overlap. ***The more similarity, the more effective the parental impact is.*** Teachers' styles also have impact, but parents usually have the most. Look at the book ***Mommy and Daddy Are Always Supposed To Say Yes ... Aren't They?*** by this author to learn to work together better as a couple. You'll also learn what to do if you're giving your child too much control.

These parenting modifications will enable your child to become a friend, not the boss of his peers.

THE ANNOYING CHILD: *"I LIKE TO BUG OTHER KIDS"*

HOW DO THESE CHILDREN BEHAVE?

The second type of child is the annoying preschooler who ruins other children's creations, and who teases and deliberately pesters. Here are some typical examples: Sean knocks over the kids' block creation. Then Sean takes the scissors from Elliott or draws on Elliott's paper. Sean may call Elliott a baby, or say, "Your hair is ugly." Molly invades Rena's space – leans on Rena or wiggles her fingers near Rena's eyes. When the kids are playing house, Molly pushes the play food off the table and grabs her classmate's play hat. Sean and Molly aren't trying to run the play like the controlling child, but are teasing to get attention.

WHAT CAN YOU DO AT THE MOMENT?

Sean comes come over to play with your son Elliot. Sean starts making silly noises and knocks over Elliot's block building, making Elliot sad. Sean calls Elliot a crybaby. ***If teased children show their distress, it encourages the annoying child. Give Elliott a phrase or two to show that he's not upset: "So?" or "Who cares?"*** He'll have to be an actor to conceal his distress until he develops a little more toughness. Tools like this are very helpful to the teased child. Again, it's best to make sure that the other child's parents are comfortable with these ideas.

Sean continues teasing Elliot.

> Elliot's parent (to Sean): *Kids don't like people who knock over their buildings or call them names. The rules in our house are that people are kind to each other. I wonder how come you knocked the building over. (If Sean doesn't say anything:) There's a better way to play and have fun.*

> Elliot's parent (to Elliot): *Tell Sean that he can say he wants to do something else, but he shouldn't just knock things down.*

> Elliot: *Sean, tell me if you want to do something else. I don't like it when people break my building.*

> Sean: *I want to do something else.*

> Elliot's parent (to Sean): *That's good, Sean, that you told Elliot that you wanted to do something else.*

> Elliot: *I'll show you all the things we have outside.*

> Sean: *OK.*

Throughout this playdate, Sean may keep upsetting Elliot.

> Elliot's parent: *Sean, it looks like I have to tell your mom and dad what you've been doing.*

Sometimes the "teaser" needs a time-out. It's hard to punish someone else's child. Sean's parents may not be happy, but it won't help his behavior if you tell them that everything went fine on the playdate. And, of course, Sean will be happier when he learns to behave so others like him and want to be with him.

In another type of situation, the kids are playing at your home. Molly starts banging the plates and cups, messing up the table Rena set for the tea party.

> Molly's parent (to Molly): *You want to play with Rena, but she's busy cooking. You want to get her to notice you and ask you to play.*

We say this because young children often don't know why they just said or did what they did. Telling them in front of their playmate helps them understand themselves and helps their playmates understand them better. It's also useful for youngsters to suggest an idea rather than just asking, "Can I play with you?" – because many youngsters will answer no.

> Molly's parent (to Molly): *Ask Rena, "How about if I make muffins?"*
>
> Molly (to Rena): *How about if I make cupcakes?*
>
> Rena: *No, thanks.*
>
> Parent (to Rena): *Molly had a good idea.*
>
> Parent (to Molly): *Ask Rena, "If you don't want me to make cupcakes, what else can I do to help?"*

Later, Molly is alternating leaning against Rena and flicking Rena with her fingers.

> Molly's parent (to Rena): *Tell Molly, "I don't want to be friends with kids who bother me. Just ask me if I want to play outside or do puzzles. I like those kids best."*
>
> Molly's parent (to Molly): *Ask Rena, "Do you want to go outside and swing on the swings?"*
>
> Molly (to Rena): *Do you want to swing on the swings?*
>
> Rena: *OK.*

WHY KIDS BEHAVE THAT WAY

Most children who tease and annoy other kids want to play with them. At home, these kids may not have enough good interaction with their parents and try to get noticed by doing bothersome things such as making the sink overflow, making loud noises, or playing with their parents' smart phones. *The pattern of being annoying to get attention can carry over to interactions with peers.* In addition, if the parents regularly try to get their child to behave by just giving "logical" reasons, she may refuse, get punished, and get angry. When preschoolers feel misunderstood and get uncomfortable, they often get silly and annoying and do irritating things such as telling their parents, "You're a poopoohead."

Children who develop a pattern of annoying others often have parents who aren't used to acknowledging their child's intense feelings. That leaves the child to deal with her difficult emotions and feel misunderstood, leading to the impulse to tease others. *These children may not care about pleasing their parents, which is an essential motivation for behaving well.*

WHAT PARENTS CAN ADJUST IN THEIR RELATIONSHIP WITH THEIR ANNOYING CHILD

If your child resists cooperating and you often threaten or use consequences, you both may be frustrated and angry. She may want to annoy you because she is always in trouble with you. *Why Do I Have To?* by this author explains how youngsters think, how to get them to cooperate, and the most effective consequences to use. Here are some more suggestions.

• **If you expect your youngster to amuse herself, it's time to revisit your parenting assumptions.** Children five and under need extensive parent involvement and monitoring. Make time to play with them, teach them, read to them, and show them that you enjoy their company. Take them on child-centered outings and involve them in your activities and chores, talking with them about what you're doing. Go to them and check on them frequently. Set them up with activities while you do brief tasks, but don't expect to get much done when they're awake. Lacking attention, they will go from one mischievous misdeed to the next, and annoying others becomes a habit.

• **Find a common interest that you and your child share – whether it's cars, dinosaurs, drawing, gardening, etc. That helps her feel you enjoy her company.**

• **Work hard to help her learn necessary skills – falling asleep, toothbrushing, doing puzzles, picking up toys, etc.** Acknowledge how difficult it is, and praise and hug her. Minimize material rewards for accomplishment. Kids should feel good about doing what we expect and pleasing us – not just cooperate to get things.

• **Discussing feelings, listening to children's feelings, and teaching them to cope with difficult moments will help children avoid or reduce annoying and provoking behavior.**

For example, your child seems angry.

Parent: *Something has made you very mad.*

If you know what it is, tell her – because then she feels you understand her and you care.

Parent: *I think you're mad because I told you to stop playing outside and come in. Let's do something fun inside, and let's plan when you can go out again.*

Or if you don't know, offer multiple choices.

Parent: *Is it because Jesse couldn't come over or because I told you I'm too busy to play?*

You can also mention how frustrated you felt as a child when you couldn't do what you wanted. You can illustrate how you told yourself things that helped.

Parent: *One day when I was five, I had to go home from my best friend Nicole's because she was going to her grandma's. I said to myself, "I'm mad because I can't stay and play. I'm going to ask my mommy when Nicole can play with me again." That helped me not to be so angry.*

But some things I told myself didn't help, like when I said, "I'm not going home. My mommy is mean and I don't like her." That didn't help. I yelled at Mommy and she gave me a time-out.

Have your child try out some ways to talk about her frustration. Let her know that Mommy and Daddy want to know how she feels. For some children, talking about feelings isn't easy.

• **Parents often tell upset kids, "Go to your room till you calm down." Remember, most kids don't know how to calm down.**

We can offer more than "take deep breaths" and "count to 10."

Parent (to child four to six years old): *Now, tell yourself, "I'm so mad, because I still want to play outside. But it's dark. What can I do inside – what can I do?"*

As for your three-year-old, teach her a calming mantra.

Kiely, age three: *"I'll be OK. I'll be OK. I'll be OK."*

Children need guidance in dealing with intense, difficult feelings. Wanting to please their parents helps them reduce or eliminate annoying behavior.

• **If your child continues to annoy her classmates, talk to the teacher and help out in the class so you can see what's going on. Have one child at a time over for playdates to help your child build good one-on-one relationships.** With your help, close supervision, and suggestions during their playdate, your child can be viewed as a nice, fun kid to play with, not just a pest. (See the following Case Study (p. 35) and the "What can you do at the moment?" section (pp. 32-33).

THE PHYSICALLY AGGRESSIVE CHILD: "GIVE ME THAT BOOK OR I'LL HIT YOU"

HOW DO THESE CHILDREN BEHAVE?

Some preschoolers and kindergartners are still grabbing, hitting, and pushing. They may hurt a child who has taken something away from them. Some are almost constantly physical with other kids – just being around kids seems to launch them into physical aggression using play swords and guns, and using their fingers as a gun. *All this physical aggression can happen until kids can solve conflicts with words.*

Cooper, age four, was always getting into trouble at preschool. He called kids "baby" or "poopoo butt," grabbed their toys, and ruined their buildings or crafts. He interrupted teachers during story time, shouted out without being called on, and led other kids into misbehavior with such ideas as "Let's throw the baby doll out of the high chair." Many of his classmates felt unsafe at school because of him. The teachers worked hard with Cooper. They supervised him closely, told him how he made the others feel, and tried to help him and the other kids express their thoughts and feelings. They gave him time-outs, and required him to leave school early unless he earned the right to stay by behaving better, but his behavior didn't improve.

Their pediatrician recommended a specialist in young children's behavior who met with Cooper's parents, Laura and Robert, and also with his teachers. The specialist asked to observe Cooper's typical time at home, including having his parents ask him to pick up his toys and talk to him about his day at school and about his behavior.

Laura and Robert both had demanding jobs. During the home visit, both parents did what they usually did – took calls and checked e-mail, expecting Cooper to amuse himself. Meanwhile, Cooper drew on the wall, squeezed toothpaste all over the sink, knocked his building over, and tore the pages out of a book. That got Laura and Robert's attention, and they punished Cooper, taking away his favorite toys and "blankie," and giving him time-outs and swats on the bottom. Cooper, feeling unimportant and angry, had increasingly become the teaser and troublemaker. **(It's also important to know that when parents use consequences that teachers can't – long time-outs, pulling kids' ears, pinching them, and spanking – children are not very responsive to the less severe consequences at school.)**

Cooper preferred to be a "bad boy" rather than an unnoticed boy. The behavior specialist advised Laura and Robert that Cooper needed definite time when his parents were available to play, talk and read to him. They began to include him while they cooked, vacuumed, or gardened. They learned how to supervise Cooper when they weren't sharing an activity with him, alternating a period of frequent involvement with a period when they were less involved but still monitoring him. They started to use more acceptable consequences (see **Why Do I Have To?** by this author).

Cooper began to want to please his parents and teachers, and be a friend to his classmates. He didn't need to be the troublemaker anymore, which was a great relief for the kids, his teachers, his parents, and most of all, for Cooper.

WHAT CAN YOU DO AT THE MOMENT?

As parents, we know we can't let kids (ours or others) hurt each other. With preschoolers and kindergartners, we should stop them by telling them, "No hitting (pushing, etc.)." Briefly take care of the one who is most hurt or most upset. Then see if you can get even a semi-accurate account of what just happened.

Anika is feeding the baby doll.

> Lysie (grabbing baby doll): *I want to feed her now!*

> Anika: *Give her back!* (Anika grabs the doll back.)

Lysie pushes Anika, who falls down.

> Anika (yelling): *I don't like you!*

Now it's time to teach both kids.

> Anika's parent (to Lysie): *It's not OK to grab or push. You should ask Anika, "Can I have the baby next?"*

> Anika's parent (to Anika): *Tell Lysie, "I'm still playing with the baby. I'll give you a turn in five minutes."*

If Lysie tries to grab the doll again:

> Anika's parent (to Anika): *Tell Lysie, "Give her back right now or I'm going to tell your mommy that you're not being nice."*

Anika (to Lysie): *I said give her back or I'll tell your mommy what you did.*

Anika's parent (to Lysie): *No more grabbing You can watch Anika play with the baby doll or you can make some pizza for all of us to eat.*

See if you can get both kids to practice what they should have said so the words become easier and more familiar.

Of course, there could be other consequences – in addition to getting children to practice what they can say to each other. Time-out (preferably in the child's bedroom) can be memorable, especially if you have your child think about the following question to help him see the parent's viewpoint: "What am I (the parent) thinking about you right now, and why am I thinking that?" At a park or playgroup, you can sit next to your child after his aggressive behavior, with your arm firmly around him, to do time-out. **Tell him that when he hurt that child, "Your fun stops." This is more effective than leaving the park or playgroup, because at the park, he still has to see the other kids playing.** You can also take something meaningful away for a day or two. Apologizing and doing something nice for the hurt child is useful as a way to make up. However, the emphasis should be on teaching kids to use words instead of physical force, and what words to use.

WHY KIDS BEHAVE THAT WAY

Many young children use physical aggression to deal with frustration or to burn off energy. They may be impatient and impulsive, or not skilled at telling others what they want. Sometimes they're physically aggressive because their parents are physically forceful, or because aggression works with their siblings.

WHAT PARENTS CAN ADJUST IN THEIR RELATIONSHIP WITH THEIR PHYSICALLY AGGRESSIVE CHILD

• **Socializing our kids means teaching them to use words to solve problems.** Parents have to teach them: It's not OK to hit – to hurt. Instead, children need to learn to "use your words." **However, we need to teach preschoolers what words to use.**

• **Make sure children get to run, play ball, climb, jump, and get outside for many hours a day – and try to have places in your home where they can jump and move.**

• **When your child is being physically aggressive, suggest words or activities that will decrease his frustration and help him to feel understood.**

Parent (to Liam): *When you're mad because you can't jump on the couch (or have to leave the park), it's not OK to hit me. Here's what you can say: "Mommy (or Daddy), I'm mad! I don't want to pick up my toys!"*

We show our younger preschoolers how to say it with intensity, to get some of the same release they feel when they hit and scream. We respond with compassion.

Parent: *Of course you're mad. You were playing and you didn't want to stop. Here's what we're going to do now … and after dinner, we can play some more.*

(Young children need your help planning for something enjoyable, to reduce their frustration.)

• **Minimize getting physical with your kids.** Physically overpowering them to force them to do what you want (e.g. strong-arming your child into his car seat) makes youngsters very angry and more likely to be physical with others. Also, look closely at eliminating spanking, swatting, and slapping our kids. Use the other consequences mentioned in this manual so you can be effective without spanking. **When we say "you may not hit" as we're hitting them, we know the message our** *kids get from that.* And parents should also try reducing roughhousing with their kids.

Now we turn to the other, very different group of children: the quiet *and* the very sensitive child.

THE QUIET, SELF-CONSCIOUS CHILD: "I DON'T WANT TO PLAY"

HOW DO THESE KIDS BEHAVE?

This quiet, self-conscious child tends to play alone and ignore other children's overtures, especially in a group or class. For example, Alexa is playing by herself, and nearby, Brittany is pouring tea for a group of stuffed animals. The teacher suggests that Brittany invite Alexa, and Brittany willingly does. But Alexa has little to say, and the play quickly falls apart.

Quiet children like Alexa may pay attention to adult-child and child-child conversations, but rarely offer comments. Alexa often plays alone. She chooses activities and focuses on them, and listens well to directions and stories. She tends to be uncomfortable answering questions, especially in a group. She probably knows the words and hand motions to all the songs and activities, but may be too self-conscious to participate at school, though she usually does them at home.

Alexa likes to go to school and tells her parents about what happened during the day in detail. *But when her teacher describes Alexa's behavior at school, her parents can see that she's not comfortable and not herself when she's there.*

WHAT CAN YOU DO AT THE MOMENT?

The most important way to help your quiet, self-conscious child is to find compatible playmates: a similar child or an easygoing, relaxed, fun child – not a bossy, teasing, or angry child. Arrange one-on-one playdates a few times a week. Teachers can have your quiet child and her friend come before or stay after school and have a chance to play and talk together at school, or parents can take the two to school together.

Parents and teachers can help by making sure your quiet child knows the day's activities, and teachers can give the child a helpful job at the beginning of the day.

Teacher: *Andrei, today we'll be making presents for our mommies and daddies with colored paper, glitter, and streamers. Then at circle time I'm going to read a book about making presents. Could you help by putting the jars of red glitter and silver glitter on each table?*

Teachers can talk to your child one-on-one and then get her permission to share her comment with the class, so she knows what's coming and feels that her comment are worthwhile.

Alexa (very quietly, to teacher): *Can we sing "On Top of Spaghetti" at circle time?*

Teacher: *Yes, we can. Is it OK if I tell the other kids about your good idea?*

Alexa: *OK.*

Teacher (to all the kids): *Alexa had a great idea for circle time. She wants to sing "On Top of Spaghetti."*

Kids: *Yay*!

Make sure you try school activities and songs at home. Borrow the school's music CDs so your child can get more relaxed with the music by singing with the family.

You or the teachers may also have to stay close to your quiet child and suggest what he can say to a playmate so he can express himself more easily and confidently.

Andrei is waiting for a friend to come over for a playdate.

Andrei's parent: *What would you like to do when Kai comes over?*

Andrei: *Could we ask him if he wants to go outside and dig in the sandbox?*

(When Kai arrives:)

Andrei's parent: *You can ask Kai what he wants to do. Don't forget to also tell him tell him what you want to do. You can say, "Kai, do you want to dig with me in the sandbox and fill up my new dump truck?"*

Andrei (quietly, but so Kai can hear him): *Want to go out in the sandbox and fill up the new dump truck with sand?*

When you're just with your child, do some fun and silly games – playing "school" or other group experiences using teddy bears as if they were the other kids in her class. See if that gets her to relax a little. Many of these children, with guidance and support, begin taking risks by answering peers or suggesting ideas. Then they will begin making friends at school.

WHY KIDS BEHAVE THAT WAY

There are many possible reasons for a child to be quiet, self-conscious, and an observer in a group. Some children's temperaments and personalities makes them uncomfortable with big groups because of noise or confusion. Some children have had very little social interaction in groups or playdates and find kids' behavior unsettling and unpredictable.

Some children have quieter, less confident parents. If parents rarely invite visitors to their home to socialize, are uncertain with others, or just have a tendency to be quiet, children may pick up that social behavior. *Occasionally a child who has been allowed too much control at home will be quiet at school, where she has to work hard to get as much control.* She'd rather wait till she gets home, where she easily runs things. If you think that's the problem, you should work on being in charge. *Other quiet children may have very dominating parents, which can cause a child to feel less confident.* (The Case Study on p. 39 shows the possible effect.)

Sometimes the child is just the very *youngest* in the group and has trouble keeping up. And children with delays such as *speech and language* may have difficulty communicating. By age four, peer skills are dependent on language development, so one lag may lead to another. If a child has had little exposure to the common language of her class, she may not try to communicate as much.

WHAT PARENTS CAN ADJUST IN THEIR RELATIONSHIP WITH THEIR CHILD WHO IS QUIET AND SELF-CONSCIOUS

• **Consider whether this style is similar to either you or your spouse as children.** If you're still predominantly quiet and self-conscious, you may be willing to work on these traits for your child's sake. If you're reserved, it's especially important to invite friends for your kids, because that helps them *and* helps you develop more friendships with other parents. You can also volunteer at your child's school or in the community. This will encourage you to interact with more people at your home and theirs. Conversations in person – or even by phone – rather than e-mailing, instant-messaging, etc., model real social interaction for your child.

• **Look at how you and your child decide what to play or do together.** Make sure you don't say yes to all of her ideas. Getting her used to explaining herself and having to talk you into playing what she wants will make it easier for her to assert herself and/or negotiate with peers.

> Alexa: *Mommy, will you build a Marble Run with me?*
>
> Mommy: *I don't know, Alexa. I think it's somewhere in the garage and we'll have to clean up the playroom to have space for it on the floor. Why do you think playing Marble Run is a good idea?*
>
> Alexa: *Because it's really fun to build and see how fast the marbles go. I'll clean up the playroom, Mommy, and then I'll help you find it.*
>
> Mommy: *That all sounds good. Now I want to play Marble Run too.*

• **Invite the teacher over early in the school year so she and your child understand each other better and feel more relaxed with each other.**

• **Relax with your child by singing, dancing, and telling jokes.** Do silly stuff at home with your child like making believe you're elephants, frogs, and butterflies, etc., so your child associates these potentially "self-conscious" preschool activities with the fun and laughter from your shared experiences at home.

• **Whenever you have a chance, lead a group of children – with your child among them – reading out loud, singing, or doing finger plays. Make sure you call on her.** If you – the person she's so comfortable with – are leading the group, she will start to become much more relaxed, playful, and willing to participate. This could be at her birthday party, a playdate or playgroup. Also arrange with the teacher for you to lead a group with her and her classmates at school.

CASE STUDY:
THE QUIET CHILD WHO DOESN'T STAND UP FOR HERSELF

The preschool teachers were worried about four-and-a-half-year-old Jillian. After a year at the preschool, she was still very quiet. She said very little to either the teachers or the children, and wanted to stay near the teachers. She rarely suggested any ideas and just went along with the other kids' suggestions. She seemed younger than her classmates, though she wasn't. Kids paid little attention to her – as if she were invisible. Her voice was quiet and hesitant, and by the time she answered the kids, they had moved on.

The teachers tried to urge her to express herself and encouraged friendships with other kids, but she remained reserved and didn't stand up for herself. When a playmate said, "I'll be the mommy and you be the kitty," Jillian complied unhappily. She didn't ask the teachers for help. When she was waiting to use the swing and another child cut ahead to take it, Jillian looked disappointed but said nothing.

The preschool teachers talked to Jillian's parents, Melanie and Paul, who said Jillian talked about her classmates and what they did, and didn't say she liked or disliked school. Jillian wasn't eager to have playdates, and Melanie, an at-home mom, was OK with that because she was busy with her two younger children. Her parents saw Jillian as happy, but as more serious, quiet and observing than their two-year-old and even their six-month-old.

The teachers recommended a consultation with a child/parent psychologist. The psychologist asked about Jillian's language development and play interests, how she played with her sibs, how much she did for herself such as dressing, toy pickup, and so forth; and about each parent's approach to child-rearing, including what consequences they used. The psychologist observed while the parents talked and played with Jillian and her sibs. The specialist had the parents ask Jillian to do things kids her age are expected to do but often resist doing, and to use their typical consequences.

The psychologist noticed that **Paul was directive, impatient, and loud, and expected Jillian to comply immediately. He didn't know how much to expect of a four-and-a-half-year-old or how to get her cooperation.** Jillian seemed uncertain around her dad. **Melanie was very different. She was very patient, babying Jillian and doing too much for her** – dressing her and even feeding her at times. This was partly due to Melanie's personality and partly

because she was so busy, that it was fastest to do things herself. Some of Melanie's overnurturing parenting was in reaction to Paul's harshness. The different styles led to tension and anger between the parents.

Her parents' styles, combined with her sensitive nature, had affected Jillian's confidence and assertiveness. Jillian had not developed the competence to do age-appropriate tasks. Neither parenting style was effective, and her parents' opposite styles and expectations – and their arguing over her – fueled her insecurity.

The psychologist guided Paul in understanding how preschoolers think, how to get them to cooperate, and age-appropriate consequences, and explained the negative effects of his impatience and yelling. The guidance to Melanie focused on clarifying what to expect of Jillian at four and a half. The parents learned to help her problem-solve at home. They made an effort to praise and encourage Jillian's ideas and opinions, even if they differed from her parents'. They started inviting playdates over, helped her come up with good play ideas, and encouraged her to present them more enthusiastically and loudly, including when they played with her. As the parents became a parenting team, Jillian began to bloom, suggest ideas, add to the conversation, and defend her rights.

• **Increase your child's confidence by asking his opinion.**

> Mommy: *Cody, do you think we should put bananas or blueberries on our cereal this morning, or do you have a different idea?*
>
> Cody: *What about bananas **and** blueberries?*
>
> Mommy: *That will be delicious!*

(And on another day:)

> Daddy: *Cody, we should keep your art supplies someplace where you can get them out yourself when you want them, as long as you put them away. Can you think of a place?*
>
> Cody: *What about keeping them on the shelf under the board games?*
>
> Daddy: *I think that will work!*

Let your child try out solutions to these and other ordinary situations. Your questions, his solutions, and the outcomes help him become more confident in offering his ideas to others, even to groups.

• **Try to be more patient with your quieter, self-conscious child.** She probably shouldn't be rushed into lots of big noisy classes or situations if they make her uncomfortable. Little by little, we ask more of her so she doesn't get stuck in her current pattern, but we do it in baby steps.

THE THIN-SKINNED CHILD WHO CAN'T STAND UP FOR HIMSELF: "THEY HURT MY FEELINGS"

HOW DO THESE KIDS BEHAVE?

The other type of "uncomfortable" child is the very emotionally sensitive, easily upset child. Like the quiet, self-conscious follower, this child also tends to follow and do what others say. **When other kids tease, ignore, or correct him he starts to look very sad and may cry** – sometimes very quietly. He even gets upset when others are the target. When he's upset, it takes him a very long time to recover. He may put his head down on the desk or pull his shirt up over his face. Many of these kids can't accept help from the teacher or peers, though everyone may be concerned. Some thin-skinned children sob, and some have trouble catching their breath.

WHAT CAN YOU DO AT THE MOMENT?

It's very important for parents to help this kind of child. Kids like this can become isolated, sad, frustrated, and angry, and perceive life as unfair. When a preschooler or kindergartner becomes so sad that he just shuts down or cries, try to help him figure out what upset him.

> Parent: *Why do you look so sad, Alan? What happened?*
>
> Alan: *Nothing.*
>
> Parent: *Did you get hurt? Or did somebody say something or do something that made you sad?*
>
> Alan: (Long pause) *Well … um … I was building a tower and Mark said my tower looked stupid.*

Multiple-choice questions can help a child figure out what the problem is and also feel that you care about him. Once you know what happened, sympathetically let him know that you can see why he's upset, encourage him to tell more about his feelings, and suggest how he could respond to the child who upset him. Try role-plays out at home in a relaxed, fun way.

> Alan's parent: *Alan, let's practice what you could say to yourself and Mark. Let's make believe your teddy bear is Mark.*
>
> Alan (sadly): *OK.*
>
> Parent (to Alan): *You can tell yourself, "Mark's not being nice, so he can't be my friend." Or, "It doesn't matter what Mark says. My tower is good."*
>
> Parent (directing speech at teddy bear): *Mark, who cares?*
>
> Parent (to Alan): *Alan can you say that?*
>
> Alan (softly): *I don't care!*
>
> Parent (speaking in a kid's voice as "Mark"): *What did you say?*
>
> Alan (louder): *Who cares!*
>
> Parent (speaking in a kid's voice as "Mark"): *OK, OK. So, do you want to build a road with me?*

If your child is the youngest in his class, consider whether he can be moved to another class, and/or have some playdates or other activities where he's not the youngest. The playdates should be fair-minded, kind, and upbeat kids.

WHY KIDS BEHAVE THAT WAY

Children may be innately, temperamentally sensitive. They don't like loud voices or anger and may even be upset by sad-sounding music. They may also be frightened or anxious from stress at home. Sad and depressed or stressed and angry parents or siblings can make the home an unhappy, scary, tension-filled place.

WHAT PARENTS CAN ADJUST IN THEIR RELATIONSHIP WITH THEIR SENSITIVE KIDS

• **Make sure you're not usually too directive or commanding with your child.** In today's society, this would handicap your child, as most children are being raised to assert themselves.

• **Parents need to be empathetic toward their children's sensitivities, commenting in a gentle manner on how sad or uncertain they seem.** You can say, "It's hard to know what to do when someone hurts your feelings and makes you feel sad." Make sure you support his expressing his hurt feelings to whoever caused them, including you. Tell him about times someone hurt your feelings. If you are willing to listen and help him – without overprotecting him – then he will be more capable with peers. You can also tell him, "Sometimes you don't want to play with Mark because he's not being a good friend." Then ask him if he wants to practice what he can say to Mark.

• **The sensitive child needs encouragement and practice when things don't go his way with family and when his playdates don't like his toys or his ideas.** Parents should role-play what he can say to others and to himself, such as: "So? Who cares?" And to himself: "It's not that important. I thought my idea was good." He also needs to learn to express himself when he's being disregarded at home. For example, Alan is talking to you and a family member interrupts. Alan needs to learn to say, "But I'm not done talking yet," or, "I'm still talking."

• **Role-play common peer situations with him at home.** For example, "It's not OK to get ahead of me in line." Act it out with your spouse or a sibling and let your young child be the audience before he's actually ready to role-play. And he can be taught to tell himself about the other kid, "Jacob still has a lot to learn."

• **Teach him to use an assertive, confident voice ("Don't push me. That's against the rule.") and, as needed, the ultimate weapon in preschool and kindergarten: "I'm telling the teacher."** And to himself, he can say, "Brandon doesn't know how to be a good friend. I like Max better."

These suggestions can help the thin-skinned, easily upset child to not collapse emotionally in such despair.

To learn more about children with uncomfortable peer relationships, see *Freeing Your Child from Anxiety* by Tamar Chansky (Three Rivers Press, an imprint of Crown Publishing, a division of Random House, 2004).

• SECTION FOUR •
HOW BEING AN "ONLY" CHILD OR HAVING SIBLINGS MAY AFFECT PEER SKILLS

Being an "only" child has an impact on a child's social skills, and so does having difficult sibling relations.

THE EFFECT OF BEING AN "ONLY" CHILD

An increasing number of families today are raising "only" children. In 1970, 4% of families raised "only" children. In 2011, 23% are raising "only" children, and the percentages are increasing.

Here are the main issues that "only" children commonly face:

• **Growing up with adults, they tend to be most comfortable in that world and much less so with peers.**

•They may be accustomed to reasoning and negotiating with adults and find it unsuccessful with peers.

•They are often used to lots of attention and lots of say, and may be surprised and unhappy – even angry – when peers won't just listen to them.

•They tend not to be skilled in initiating play, turn-taking, and compromising; they may give up too easily or get angry.

WHAT PARENTS OF "ONLY" CHILDREN CAN DO TO MAKE THEIR KIDS MORE SOCIALLY COMFORTABLE AND SKILLED

• Make sure your child has time with other kids, individually and in groups. Babysit others with yours. Take other kids on outings with your family so your child isn't always the center of your attention.

• **Don't treat your "only" child as a peer (as a third adult)** by letting her decide on what your family is having for dinner, where to go on outings, or which parent should read to her. Parents should decide for younger preschoolers. For older preschoolers, make sure you explain what your thinking is. Let her voice her ideas, but make sure you don't always go along with them.

• Be selfish enough to not let your child always tell you what you'll play with her, what table the family will eat at, etc. Otherwise, she'll learn the hard way that she won't be catered to by peers.

• Have your child help you with cooking, chores, gardening, etc., **so you're teaching her** what needs to be done.

• Help in her preschool and kindergarten (and beyond) so you learn more about her age-mates, what to expect, how she's doing, and what kids she's friendly with. This helps with her ability to build social contacts, and it's easier for your child to tell you about her day when you've spent some time helping out in her class.

You can certainly raise socially skilled "only" children. It helps to know from the beginning those things you should pay attention to in your child-rearing.

THE EFFECT OF SIBLING RELATIONS ON YOUR CHILD'S PEER SKILLS

It is widely accepted that children who grow up with siblings are more comfortable with other children. *Most siblings learn the basics of sharing and compromising.* The quality of the sibling relations depends on many factors – age differences, temperament, gender, activity level, parents' own experiences growing up with their sibs, as well as their skills in parenting. If your preschooler or kindergartner is having difficulties getting along with his peers, take a close look at the way he gets along with his own siblings. *Sibling relationships can strongly impact peer relations.*

It's natural for the older sibling to have more ideas and tools to control most interactions with their younger sibs, including their play. It's also natural for younger children to want more say as they get older, and older sibs are often not willing to give that up. Younger sibs usually adore their older sibs and crave their attention *even if* they're being treated badly by the older sib. Older sibs commonly get annoyed at the younger sib's persistence and feel "bugged" and unable to get away.

It's wonderful when they get along the majority of the time, but when they don't, look for patterns that can harm the personality development and self-esteem of either sib. *Although parents have been told "just let them*

work it out themselves," damaging patterns can develop when we don't intervene enough. We can't possibly handle every one or even most of their interactions. But if we don't handle enough and give them both insight into why they're doing what they're doing, opportunities to express their difficult feelings about each other, and tools to interact better, we allow damaging patterns to develop. In the following examples, the "hurt" sib can become "one down" in his peer relations or become the dominator imitating his hurtful sibling. *Here are some common patterns and ways we can help our children.*

• **Does Will (the older sib) seem frequently resentful of Austin – demeaning, teasing, or hurting him, possibly out of jealousy ("You're a baby" or "You don't know anything")?** Does Austin feel like Will is mean and doesn't like him? (This can make Austin feel less confident and can cause him to either try to dominate peers *or* just be glad anyone will play with him.) Help Will understand where his feelings are coming from. Is Will jealous? Does Will feel that Austin gets most of the attention or too much leniency? See if you are favoring one sib. Make sure you have some one-on-one time with each and try to empathize with both. Help Will know what he can say to you when he's upset and what he can say to Austin: "I have to do my third-

grade things now. I'll play with you after dinner. Ask Mom what you can do now." Show Austin what he can say: For example, "Mommy/Daddy said that when you do that to me, I have to tell them."

• **Does one sib retaliate physically against the other?** This could be Rosie, the younger, or Marisa, the older, whichever is more physical. Does this make Rosie, the hurt one, cry and come to you for help? (This can result in Rosie's being meeker *or* being physical with peers due to frustration and resentment.) Talk to Marisa about the reasons for her physical aggression. Make sure you teach the rules about not hurting each other and the consequences, such as both girls having to explain why the hurtful one did what she did. Give Marisa the words to say instead of hurting: "I don't want you to follow me everywhere." Or: "Could you draw me two pictures?" Or: "When the timer goes off, I'll be able to play with you for a little while." Teach Rosie to say, "Remember what Mommy and Daddy said. There's no hitting or hurting in our house." Have them practice the words a lot.

• **Does one sib use the other as a servant/slave?** Usually the older one, Isabella, will give what looks like attention to the sib, Gabriel, but mostly so Gabriel will follow orders or do Isabella's jobs. For example, the parent tells Isabella to wipe off the table and Isabella gets Gabriel to do it. Tell each child in front of the other why each child is doing what he or she is doing and what you think they should do about it. What can Gabriel do or say? If Gabriel continues to be the regular and frequent servant, you'll need to explain more to each child, and ultimately prevent both from interacting that way as often as possible. If you think it will be helpful, you can have the "servant" give the "boss" several tasks to do for the "servant." You'll have to supervise this consequence closely.

• **Does the older sib, Oliver, fool the younger sib, Grace, into letting Oliver have his way by making it sound like a great idea?** This can make Grace, who can't outmaneuver Oliver yet, feel resentful, helpless, and unfairly treated. Then Grace may try the same thing with peers or submit to what peers say. As in the previous example, make sure both sibs hear your explanation of why the other is doing this and keep your eyes and ears open to intervene. A valuable "sibling problem" consequence is to have the "fooled" sibling choose something of importance to the "mastermind" so the *parent* can take it away and keep it for a few days or a week, depending on the age of the "mastermind." ***Be sure both siblings know this beforehand.***

To help change any of these harmful sibling patterns, make sure each child has enough time with you or your spouse and with his peers so he is not forced to put up with damaging behavior from the sib. Work on the damaging pattern until you see progress. And add to your parenting philosophy the guideline tha*t older sibs should be expected to spend some respectful time with their younger sibs each day – a responsibility that comes with the increasing privileges of age.*

WHEN MORE HELP IS NEEDED

When you and your child's teachers have done all you can and your young child is still having problems getting along with other youngsters, *here are the other avenues to explore. Are social skills a problem for you?* If so, read self-help books, do online research with reliable sources, or consider consulting a mental health professional. Notice whether *your child's preschool or kindergarten teacher* is friendly, enthusiastic, warm, loving, and knowledgeable in teaching kids how to make friends. Consider also whether the school's philosophy focuses enough on teaching social skills. (The book *Developmentally Appropriate Practices* (www.naeyc. org) helps parents know how to evaluate their children's preschool, daycare, and elementary school teachers and programs from infancy to eight-year-olds.)

There are several books that can be helpful to read to your child. The following four help young children understand what happens when they try various ways to play with other kids: *I Want to Play, I Can't Wait, I Want It,* and *My Name Is Not Dummy,* all by Elizabeth Crary, (Parenting Press, 1996). *Making Friends* by Fred Rogers is also useful (Putnam and Grosset Group, a Paperstar book, 1996). For parents of elementary school children, see *Friends Forever: How Parents Can Help Their Kids Make and Keep Good Friends,* by Fred Frankel (Jossey-Bass, an imprint of John Wiley & Sons, 2010). *Other options to consider are social skills (or friendship) groups usually led by mental health or parenting guidance professionals,* or several sessions with a child

psychologist or child behavior specialist. They can meet with your youngster *and* guide you.

• CONCLUSION •

All parents want their children to develop good social skills and learn to get along with peers. Make sure your child spends enough time with other children. Learn how to guide him in approaching other kids, asking them to play, keeping the play going harmoniously, and handling rejection.

Parents also need to be aware of any developing social difficulties. If your child tells you that no one wants to play with him, check with his teachers and friends' parents to find out what's actually happening. Use the guidance in this manual when he's having social problems because of **his** behavior **or his playmates' behavior.** Your child needs your support in developing his social skills and getting through hard times. These parenting tools and insights will help you know how to support your child in making friends and building the foundation for a lifetime of better relationships.

❖ *"Kindergarten teachers wish that more children began elementary school with better social skills, because these are so important for success in kindergarten and beyond. **But many parents are uncertain about how to teach their child to be a good friend. Dr. Rothenberg has once again come to the rescue of parents and children.** The children's story is fascinating and realistic. The parents' section explains how to teach youngsters the basic social skills as well as how to deal with peer problems. The book will give parents the words and the confidence to help their children become socially skilled. **Children and parents will both want to read their sections of this book over and over."***

— Mary Kay Stranik, MS; Parenting Program Consultant and a parent and grandparent, Minneapolis, MN

GUIDELINES FOR TEACHING PRESCHOOLERS AND KINDERGARTNERS HOW TO BECOME GOOD FRIENDS

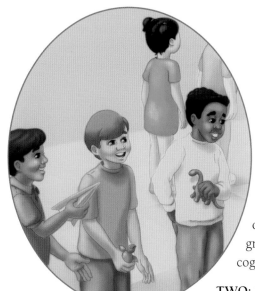

The following guidelines highlight the essentials of building good friendships and dealing with social difficulties.

ONE: *How Your Child Can Have Enough Time With Other Kids*
Most preschoolers and kindergartners need help learning skills to get along with their peers. They will have more experience if they are around other youngsters many times a week – on playdates, at parks, and in playgroups. Young children should attend preschool. The social, emotional, and cognitive benefits can be enormous. (See p. 26.)

TWO: *The Way You Are With Your Children Teaches Important Peer Skills*
When you play with your child, don't always let her decide and control everything. Make sure you tell her how her behavior affects you – what pleases and displeases you. You can also teach her to take turns with you in conversation. These are all related to what kind of friend she'll be. (See p.27.)

THREE: *Practice Common Peer Situations With Your Child*
You can teach him how to break the ice, how to explain his play ideas, how to take turns, and what to do if he is being rejected by other kids. (See pp. 28-29.)

FOUR: *What To Do When Your Child Says, "No One Wants To Play With Me"*
Make sure you ask about both sides of the situation – how she behaved **and** how the other child behaved. Most young children tend to think the other child is totally to blame. We can best help if she doesn't just continue to conclude that it is the other child's fault. It's best not to be extreme by either just taking your child's side or by telling her it was her fault. Let's help her look at both sides. (See p. 29.)

FIVE: *When Your Child Is Bossy*
Bossy children want other kids to do what they say. In addition to teaching your child how to respect and value other kids' ideas, make sure you're not modeling an extreme parenting approach – authoritarian or permissive – either of which can lead to a bossy child. Make sure he's also not getting away with dominating or being dominated by a sibling. (See pp. 30-32.)

SIX: *When Your Child Is Annoying*
Annoying children often like to pester and tease to be noticed. In addition to teaching your child how else to play with kids besides irritating them, make sure you're spending enough time involved with her. Some annoying kids have learned that to get enough attention at home, they have to be aggravating. (See pp. 32-34, 35.)

SEVEN: *When Your Child Is Physically Aggressive*
Physically aggressive kids take things from and hurt other kids. Some don't have enough outlets for their energy, and some haven't been taught how to put their feelings into words. Most need to be told what words to say. Some are hurting others because of too much roughhousing at home, and others because their parents are being too physical with them – carrying or dragging them fighting you into time-out, etc. Physically overpowering preschoolers and kindergartners usually leads to their being physically aggressive toward others. (See pp. 34-37.)

EIGHT: *When Your Child Is Quiet And Self-Conscious*

Quiet, self-conscious children are often observers and very uncomfortable in the spotlight. They need to know – and maybe even practice – what's coming next. They need our patience as we help them take baby steps. They especially benefit from being with children who are mellow and friendly. Teach him how to express his ideas. Make sure your child's speech and language development isn't interfering with his ability to socialize with other children. (See pp. 37-40.)

NINE: *When Your Child Is Thin-Skinned And Can't Stand Up For Herself*

This child's feeling are easily hurt. She's very bothered when others are unkind to her, and may cry or shut down. Be empathetic with her, but guide her to not take others' comments so personally. Teach her some responses like "Who cares?" and coach her in acting tougher than she feels. Give her practice in expressing and defending her position. (See pp. 40-41.)

TEN: *When Your Child Is An Only Child*

There are many things parents of only children can do so their child is comfortable with peers. These include arranging frequent playdates, having other children join your family on outings, and babysitting other children. These all help give your child much more experience and comfort with children. In addition, make sure you don't defer to your child in so many of the family decisions that he expects to be the third adult in the family. (See p. 42.)

ELEVEN: *When Your Child's Sibling Relationships Are Damaging Her Peer Friendships*

When one sibling is regularly demeaning, controlling, frightening, and/or hurting the other sibling, there can be a negative impact on both siblings. Usually the worst impact is on the one at the receiving end. However, the perpetrator may develop problems such as becoming too controlling and insensitive. She will need other outlets for her frustration, anger, and possibly jealousy. The sib who is on the receiving end may become less confident because of her sib, or may imitate the perpetrator and become controlling with her peers. (See pp. 42-44.)

TWELVE: *When More Help Is Needed For Your Child To Be Successful With Friends*

Look at your own social skills to see what kind of role model you are. Be a partner with your child's teacher so you're a team helping your child's social development. Make sure the teacher and the school's philosophy are the right fit for your child. Parents may also need to do more targeted research, enroll their child in a social skills group, or consult a mental health professional. (See p. 44.)

❖ *"Dr. Annye Rothenberg has done it again – clearly helping parents and children understand what gets in the way when building peer relationships and what works.*
In the story, children can see from the words and expressive illustrations how their behavior impacts others and how parents stepping in to help in a specific way can make a difference. The parents' guide thoroughly explains the reasons for these difficulties, along with detailed descriptions of how to respond, both preventively and as the situations arise. **This is a true gem in the parenting and young child literature."**

— Linda Stewart, PhD, LMFT; young child and
family therapist and a parent, Menlo Park, CA

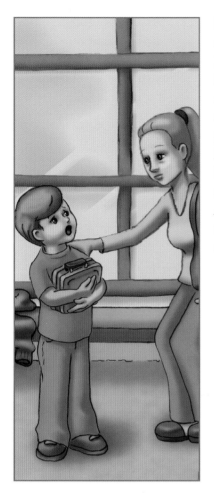

B. ANNYE ROTHENBERG, Ph.D., *author*, has been a child/parent psychologist and a specialist in child rearing and development of young children for more than 25 years. Her parenting psychology practice is in Redwood City, CA, and she is a frequent speaker to parent groups. She is also an adjunct clinical assistant professor of pediatrics at Stanford University School of Medicine and consults to pediatricians and teachers. Dr. Rothenberg was the founder/director of the Child Rearing parenting program in Palo Alto, CA, and is the author of the award-winning book *Parentmaking* (Banster Press, 1982, 1995) and other parenting education books for parenting guidance professionals. Her first four books in this award-winning series for preschoolers, kindergartners, and their parents are *Mommy and Daddy Are Always Supposed To Say Yes … Aren't They?* (2007), *Why Do I Have To?* (2008), *I Like To Eat Treats* (2009) and *I Don't Want To Go To The Toilet* (2011). She is the mother of one grown-up son.

BONNIE BRIGHT, *illustrator,* is achieving her lifelong goal of illustrating children's books. As a young girl, growing up in the mountains above Malibu, CA, Bonnie would create tiny story books about the size of your thumbnail. She also has a lifelong love for volleyball as the daughter of two Olympians, and she herself has competed at a high level. When she was offered a scholarship to play volleyball at UC Santa Barbara in 1984, she jumped at the chance to combine her two passions: volleyball and fine arts. She later studied illustration at Cal State University, Long Beach. Since then, Bonnie has illustrated many books, including *I Love You All The Time*, *The Tangle Tower,* and *Surf Angel.* Bonnie strives to make each book better than the last and to achieve her ultimate goal of bringing her imagination to life. You can visit her web site to see more examples of her work: *www.brightillustration.com*

ACKNOWLEDGEMENTS

The author is extremely grateful to *SuAnn and Kevin Kiser* for their continuing and outstanding critiques and collaboration on the children's story and to *Caroline Grannan* for her thorough and excellent editing of the parents' manual. *Cathleen O'Brien* has again shown her terrific creativity and amazing patience in the book design she has achieved. *Bonnie Bright's* work as an illustrator has been the best and we look forward to our future collaboration.

Many colleagues were willing to spend time providing thoughtful and thorough reviews of the children's story and the parents' guidance section. We are most grateful for the time and efforts of: *Mary Kay Stranik, M.S.*, *Family Program Consultant,* Minneapolis, MN; *Karina Garcia-Barbera, Ph.D., Director, Beresford Montessori Schools,* San Mateo and Redwood City, CA; *Brenda Roberts, Owner,* and *Elisa Barrett, Director*, *The Roberts School*, Menlo Park, CA; *Mary Ornellas, Director*, and *Sharon Dick, Teacher, St. Matthias Preschool*, Redwood City, CA; *Susan Kelly, Former Director, St. Paul's Nursery School*, Burlingame, CA; *Jamie Holden, Director, Trinity Presbyterian Nursery School and Parent Educator*, San Carlos, CA; *Gerry-louise Robinson, Kindergarten Teacher, The Harker School*, San Jose, CA; and *Linda Stewart, Ph.D., Marriage and Family Therapist*, Menlo Park, CA.

We are also indebted to the following San Francisco Bay Area pediatricians for their valuable comments: *Devi Ananda, M.D.*, Daly City, CA; *Howard Chow, M.D., ABC Pediatrics*, San Mateo, CA; *Monica Kenney, M.D., Hospital Drive Pediatrics*, Mountain View, CA; *Sonia Nader, M.D., Menlo Medical Clinic*, Menlo Park, CA; and *Mark Showen, M.D., Peninsula Pediatric Medical Group*, San Mateo, CA.

Be sure to read Dr. Annye Rothenberg's other All-In-One Books.

Mommy and Daddy Are Always Supposed to Say Yes...Aren't They?

A STORY FOR CHILDREN—Like many preschoolers, Alex insists that his parents should always let him have what he wants. Right now! When he plays the parent in a fun role reversal, he begins to see things differently. Alex learns that even when Mom and Dad say no, they still love him ... a lot. **INCLUDES A PARENT MANUAL—*Why don't children get the message about who's the parent?*** How to give your child just enough say. How do you deal realistically with the differences between your parenting and your spouse's? This manual includes all this and more.

Why Do I Have To?

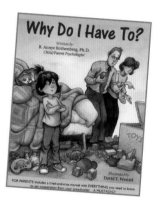

A STORY FOR CHILDREN—Sophie wonders why there are so many rules and why her parents want her to follow them. This story teaches your preschoolers just what you want them to learn. **INCLUDES A PARENT MANUAL**—Provides the keys to how preschoolers think. It teaches how to make it easier for your children to do what you ask, and offers improved popular consequences and new, more effective ones. ***This manual clears up much of the conflicting advice that parents hear.***

I Like To Eat Treats

A STORY FOR CHILDREN—Jack doesn't see why he can't eat whatever he wants. His parents decide to teach him what the many kinds of healthy foods are for. As Jack and his parents walk through the supermarket, and plan dinner for their friends, Jack really starts to understand. ***This story will actually impact your young child's understanding of nutrition.*** **INCLUDES A PARENT MANUAL** —***Gives parents realistic guidance on the most common food questions, such as: How do you get your children to eat food that's good for them? What about picky eaters? How do we change the overeater's habits and encourage our sedentary child to be more active?*** This guidebook will give you many new tools in this important area of lifelong health.

I Don't Want to Go to the Toilet

TWO STORIES FOR CHILDREN — Katie doesn't want to stop playing to go peepee in the toilet. Ben doesn't want to let his poop out in the toilet. ***In two motivating, enlightening, and reassuring stories, the children successfully overcome their resistance.*** **INCLUDES A PARENT MANUAL** — Learn how youngsters think about toilet training and how to motivate those that are uninterested, reluctant, and/or fearful. ***Parents will discover how to make toilet training easier resulting in their relief and their children's pride in being trained.***

To order these books: visit www.PerfectingParentingPress.com where you can order online *or* call (810) 388-9500 (M-F 9-5 ET). These 40 to 48 page books are $9.95 each.
Also available at www.Amazon.com.

And look for Dr. Rothenberg's sixth book in this series for preschoolers, kindergartners and their parents, *I'm Getting Ready for Kindergarten*, available in 2013.